DETECTIVE
DAN

VIVIAN FRENCH

ILLUSTRATED BY DANIEL DUNCAN

BLOOMSBURY EDUCATION

BLOOMSBURY EDUCATION
Bloomsbury Publishing Plc
50 Bedford Square, London, WC1B 3DP, UK

BLOOMSBURY, BLOOMSBURY EDUCATION and the Diana logo
are trademarks of Bloomsbury Publishing Plc

First published in Great Britain in 2004 by A& C Black, an imprint of
Bloomsbury Publishing Plc

This edition published in 2020 by Bloomsbury Publishing Plc

Text copyright © Vivian French, 2004
Illustrations copyright © Damien Barlow, 2020 in the style of Daniel Duncan

Packaged for Bloomsbury by Plum5 Limited

Vivian French has asserted her right under the Copyright,
Designs and Patents Act, 1988, to be identified as Author of this work

A catalogue record for this book is available from the British Library

ISBN: PB: 978-1-4729-6730-5;
ePDF: 978-1-4729-6731-2; ePub: 978-1-4729-6729-9

2 4 6 8 10 9 7 5 3 1

Printed and bound by CPI Group (UK) Ltd, Croydon, CR20 4YY

All papers used by Bloomsbury Publishing Plc are natural, recyclable products from wood grown in well-managed
forests. The manufacturing processes conform to the environmental regulations of the country of origin

To find out more about our authors and books visit www.bloomsbury.com and sign up for our newsletters

CONTENTS

For Ross

CHAPTER ONE

Dan and Billy were best friends. They walked to school together every morning. Every afternoon they ran home together. They did everything together.

One Monday afternoon Dan came out of school very slowly.

"What's the matter, Dan?" his mum asked.

"Someone threw his lunch box on the floor," Billy told her.

Mum said, "Maybe it just fell off the shelf."

"Mrs Harper said Dan was untidy," Billy said.

"Yes," said Dan. "And I'm *not* untidy!"

Dan stamped crossly all the way home.

On Tuesday afternoon Dan came out of school even more slowly.

"What's the matter, Dan?" his mum asked.

"Someone threw his lunch box on the floor *again*," said Billy.

"I'm sure they didn't mean to," said Mum. "Did you eat your sandwiches?"

"No," said Dan. "I didn't feel hungry."

"Mrs Harper says Dan is getting *very* untidy," Billy told Mum.

"Yes," Dan said. "And she said that I shouldn't talk to Minnie!"

"Is that the school cat?" Mum asked.

"Yes." Dan frowned. "It's not fair. I don't mean to talk to Minnie, but Minnie always comes to talk to me!"

Dan stamped crossly all the way home again.

On Wednesday afternoon Dan and Billy rushed out of school.

"Someone nibbled Dan's sandwiches!" Billy told Mum.

"Yes," said Dan. "Someone threw my lunch box on to the floor. Someone threw everything out of it. Someone nibbled one of my sardine sandwiches, and I'm *hungry!*"

"What did Mrs Harper say?" asked Mum.

"I didn't tell her," Dan said.

"Why not?" Mum asked.

"She was cross," Dan said. "Minnie came into the classroom with me."

"Mrs Harper said Dan let her in, but he didn't." Billy said. "Minnie just followed him."

"We'd better have a great big tea," said Mum.

"With extra big sardine sandwiches!" said Dan.

CHAPTER TWO

On Thursday morning Dan walked slowly along the path.

"I think I should hide my lunch box today," he told Billy. "Then no one can eat my sardine sandwiches."

"You haven't got sardine sandwiches today, Dan," Mum said. "I had to make you cheese instead."

Billy suddenly stopped.

"I know!" he said. "I'll be a detective! I'll look for clues. I'll find out who pushed your lunch box off the shelf and tell Mrs Harper. Then she won't blame you."

"*Yes!*" said Dan, and they ran all the way to school.

Dan and Billy ran into the playground.

"Look!" said Billy. "There's Minnie!"

Dan called, "Minnie! Puss, puss, puss!"

Minnie came running. She ran in and out of Dan's legs, and round and round his school bag. But when he tried to pick her up she wriggled and struggled.

Mrs Harper walked past them.

"Now, Dan," she said. "I don't want Minnie in school. Put her down, please."

Dan put Minnie down, and she
ran away at once.

"Why doesn't she like me today?"
Dan asked.

"I'll find out!" Billy told him.
"I'm a detective!"

16

"You've got to find out about my lunch box first," Dan said.

When it was time for lessons Dan and Billy hurried inside.

They put their lunch boxes on the shelf outside the classroom, and sat down at their table for quiet reading time.

"Look out for clues!" Billy whispered.

Dan nodded.

"No whispering!" Mrs Harper said.

Billy put his hand up.

"Please may I go to the toilet?" he asked.

Mrs Harper frowned. "Do you have to, Billy?"

"Yes, Mrs Harper," Billy said.

"What were you doing?" Dan whispered when Billy came back.

"Looking for clues," Billy whispered. "You go next!"

Dan put his hand up.

"Please may I go to the toilet?" he asked.

Mrs Harper frowned again. "Do you really have to go?"

Dan nodded.

"Did you see anything?" Billy whispered when Dan came back.

"My lunch box is still there," Dan whispered back.

Mrs Harper folded her arms. "Billy and Dan," she said. "I do *not* like whispering in my classroom! You two can stay inside at playtime!"

Billy smiled. "Thank you, Mrs Harper," he said.

Mrs Harper looked at him in surprise.

"What are you two up to?" she asked.

"Nothing, Mrs Harper," Billy said.

"Billy's a detective," Dan explained. "He's going to find out who's been throwing my lunch box on to the floor."

"I see," Mrs Harper said. "Well, no more whispering! And you can sit in here and read *quietly* at playtime."

CHAPTER THREE

When it was playtime Dan got his book and sat down. Billy sat down until Mrs Harper had gone out, and then he jumped up again.

"Let's look for fingerprints," he said.

"How?" Dan asked.

Billy thought for a moment. "We'll put chalk dust on all the lunch boxes," he said. "Then we'll see everybody's fingerprints!"

"Won't it be messy?" Dan asked.

"We need to find a clue," Billy told him.

"OK," said Dan.

Billy picked up the board rubber, and dusted chalk dust over the lunch boxes.

"There!" Billy said. "Now we'll see *everybody's* fingerprints!"

At dinner time Billy and Dan watched carefully as everybody else collected their boxes.

"*Yuck!*" said Molly. "My lunch box is all dusty!"

Atchoo!

"*Atchooo!*" sneezed Ben. "So is mine!"

All the children began blowing at the chalk dust.

"*Atchoo! Atchoo! Atchoo!*" they sneezed.

Mrs Harper came to see what was going on.

"Dan!" she said crossly. "Is this something to do with you and Billy?"

Dan looked at Billy. Billy looked at the floor.

"We were looking for

fingerprints," Dan explained.

Mrs Harper frowned her most terrible frown. "I think," she said, "you two had better stop being detectives *right now!*"

At the end of the afternoon Dan and Billy walked out of school very slowly indeed.

Mum was waiting at the gate.

"What's the matter now?" she asked. "Did somebody eat your sandwiches again?"

"No," Dan said. "Nobody took my lunch box today."

"Mrs Harper was very, very, very cross," Billy said.

Dan nodded.

"We had to stay in at dinner time," Billy said.

"Mrs Harper didn't read us a story in the afternoon," Dan said.

"Everyone had dusty jumpers," Billy said. "So they were cross too."

"It's not fair," said Dan, and he stamped all the way home. Billy walked home behind him.

CHAPTER FOUR

On Friday morning Dan plodded along very slowly to school.

"Cheer up," Mum said. "I made you an extra-big sardine sandwich today."

Dan didn't cheer up.

"I'll be a detective again!" Billy said. "I'll find out about your lunch box!"

"No," Dan said. "I don't like that game. I don't like it at all!"

Dan didn't cheer up when Minnie came to meet him in the playground. He didn't cheer up when he went inside.

He put his lunch box on the shelf, and sat down at his table with a sigh.

"Cheer up, Dan," said Mrs Harper.

Dan didn't answer. He picked up his book for quiet reading.

Billy looked at Dan, and then he picked up his book too.

Dan was very quiet all morning. When it was time for dinner he stayed sitting at his table. Billy stayed too.

"Come along, you two," said Mrs Harper. "Get your lunch boxes and zoom down to the dinner hall!"

"I'll get your lunch box, Dan," Billy said. He went out of the door, and stopped dead.

There was only one lunch box left on the shelf.

"Mrs Harper!" Billy shouted, "Dan's lunch box has gone again!"

Mrs Harper found Dan's empty lunch box by the waste bin.

Dan found his carton of drink behind a chair.

Billy found Dan's apple and biscuit under a table.

There was no sign of Dan's extra-big sardine sandwich anywhere.

"Dear me," Mrs Harper said. "Dan, I think you'd better have a school dinner."

"You can share my sandwiches," Billy said.

"No thank you," said Dan.

CHAPTER FIVE

After dinner Mrs Harper asked
everyone to sit down. She asked
if anyone had taken Dan's
sandwich. All the children shook
their heads.

"What kind of sandwich was it,
Dan?" Mrs Harper asked.

"Sardine," said Dan.

Everyone made a face.

"No one likes sardines except
Dan," Billy said.

"Is that true?" asked Mrs Harper.

Everyone nodded.

Mrs Harper looked at Dan. "Well, Dan! I don't know what to say. Maybe we do need a detective after all!"

Dan didn't answer. He was looking through the open classroom door.

"Are you listening to me, Dan?" Mrs Harper asked.

Dan suddenly smiled a huge smile. "I know who ate my sandwich!" he said. "It was *Minnie*!"

Mrs Harper shook her head. "Oh no, Dan. I'm sure she didn't!"

"Yes!" said Dan. "She liked me on Monday. On Tuesday she followed me into school. On Wednesday my sandwich was nibbled. But she didn't like me yesterday, and yesterday I had a cheese sandwich. Today I had sardines again, and she *did* like me." Dan looked sad.

"That's what I thought. It isn't me she likes, though. It's my

sardine sandwiches! Look!" And he
pointed.

Mrs Harper looked. So did Billy.
So did all the children in the class.

Minnie was up on the lunch box shelf. She was walking in and out of the empty boxes, sniffing. Suddenly, she stopped.

"That's my box!" Dan whispered.

Minnie pushed at the box with her paw.

CRASH!

It fell on to the floor, and opened. Minnie jumped down and climbed inside. She was purring loudly.

"Well, I never," said Mrs Harper. "Well done, Detective Dan!"

The children cheered.

"Next week you'd better keep your lunch box *inside* the classroom!" Mrs Harper said.

Dan nodded.

Mrs Harper smiled at him.

"I'm sorry I said you were untidy. And I'm sure Minnie is too!"

At the end of Friday afternoon Dan came jumping out of school.

"You've cheered up!" Mum said.

"*Yes!*" said Dan. "Come on, Billy! Let's *run!*"

"OK," said Billy. He looked at Mum.

"Did you know?" he said. "Dan's the best detective *ever!*"

And Dan and Billy ran all the way home together.

READING ZONE!

WHAT DO YOU THINK?

Did you have any ideas about what was happening to Dan's lunchbox before you found out it was Minnie?

What clues did you find in the story?

Did you suspect any of the characters?

Do you think there were enough clues to help you figure it out like Dan did?

READING ZONE!

QUIZ TIME

Can you remember the answers to these questions?

- Why did Dan stamp crossly all the way home on Monday?

- What was in the sandwich that someone had nibbled?

- Why were lots of children sneezing when they picked up their lunchboxes on Thursday?

- Where did Mrs Harper find Dan's empty lunchbox on Friday?

- How did Minnie know if Dan had sardine sandwiches or not?

READING ZONE!

GET CREATIVE

Why not design your
own sandwich?

Think about the bread you would
like to use, and what fillings and
toppings you would like to add.

What shape you would cut
your sandwich into?

You could draw a detailed
picture and label it to show what
your sandwich would look like,
or maybe an adult could help
you to make one for lunch!